THE MARE

SETH CHRISTIAN MARTEL

graphic mundi

Library of Congress Cataloging-in-Publication Data

Names: Martel, Seth Christian, 1979- author.
Title: The mare / Seth Christian Martel.
Description: University Park, Pennsylvania : Graphic Mundi, [2023] | Audience: Grades 10–12
Summary: "A juvenile fiction coming-of-age story in graphic novel format, exploring issues of self-doubt and restlessness in the late teenage years"—Provided by publisher.
Identifiers: LCCN 2022030996 | ISBN 9781637790465 (paperback)
Subjects: LCSH: Teenage girls—Comic books, strips, etc. | Munchausen syndrome by proxy—Comic books, strips, etc. | Coming of age—Comic books, strips, etc. | Self-doubt—Comic books, strips, etc. | LCGFT: Graphic novels. | Coming-of-age comics. | Paranormal comics.
Classification: LCC PZ7.7.M366 Mar 2023 | DDC 741.5/973—dc23/eng/20220721
LC record available at https://lccn.loc.gov/2022030996

Printed in Lithuania by BALTO Print
Published by The Pennsylvania State University Press,
University Park, PA 16802-1003

10 9 8 7 6 5 4 3 2 1

Graphic Mundi is an imprint of The Pennsylvania State University Press.

The Pennsylvania State University Press is a member of the Association of University Presses.

It is the policy of The Pennsylvania State University Press to use acid-free paper. Publications on uncoated stock satisfy the minimum requirements of American National Standard for Information Sciences—Permanence of Paper for Printed Library Material, ANSI Z39.48-1992.

1

Sour Times

I'm just so tired.

Going to bed used to be my favorite part of the day. Pajamas and warm blankets pulled up to my nose -- it really was the best.

For the last three weeks, when I close my eyes, a suffocating force holds me down against my bed. Icy cold fingers rake my skin. I try to speak and only silent screams come out.
I *know* I'm asleep. I absolutely *know* it. But trying to wake up feels like grasping for those jail cell keys that are just out of reach. My brain doesn't have control of my body, and I feel like a hostage in my own bed.

I'm not scared... anymore. I read about sleep paralysis at the library. I know what's coming when I drift off, like a Groundhog Day of torture. I'm just so tired.
The night feels angry and relentless, and I'm just along for the ride. All until...

...I finally wake up.

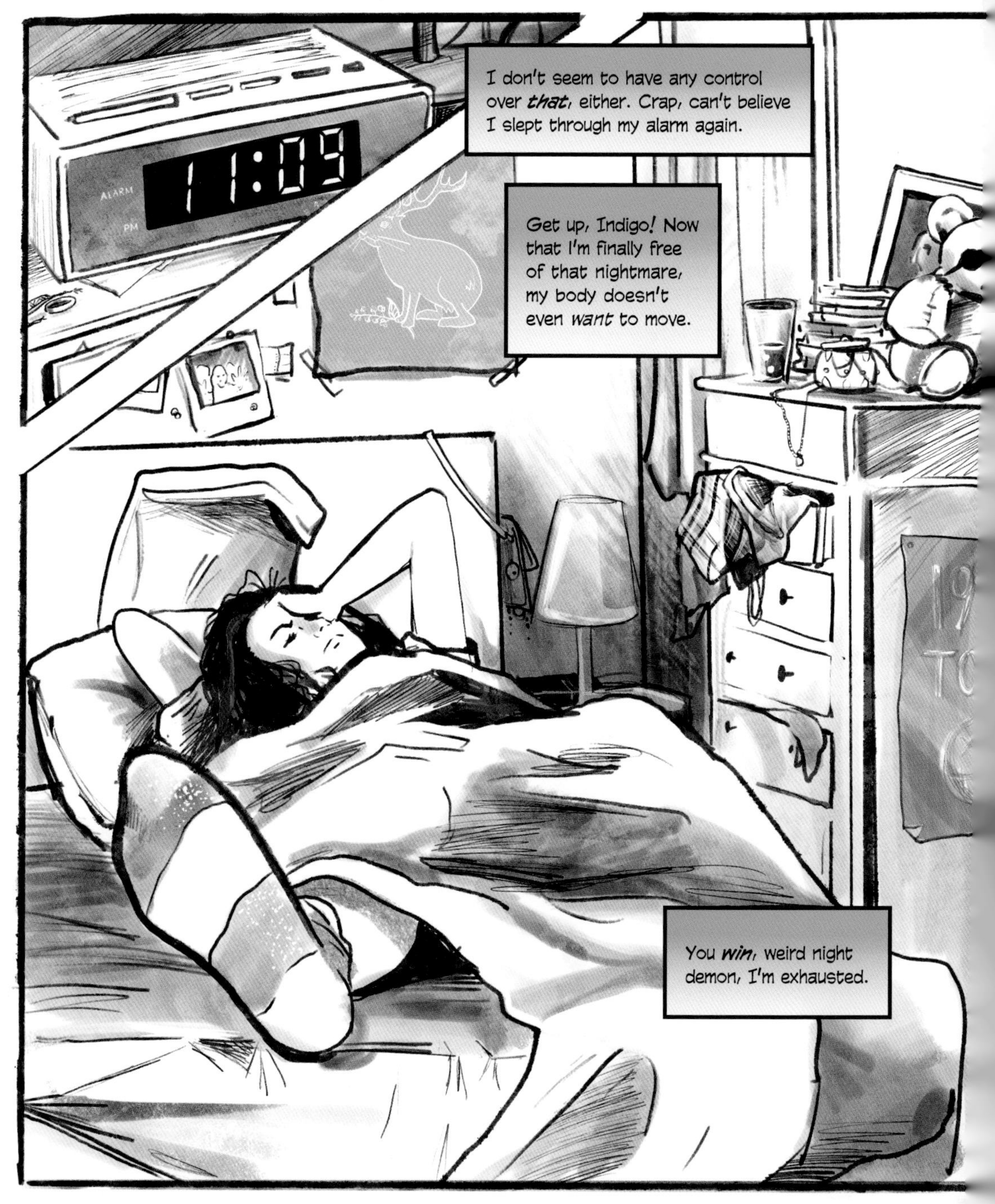
I don't seem to have any control over *that*, either. Crap, can't believe I slept through my alarm again.
11:09
Get up, Indigo! Now that I'm finally free of that nightmare, my body doesn't even *want* to move.
You *win*, weird night demon, I'm exhausted.

Ugh, not again.
Hey, Dad! C'mon, let's get to bed.
Why do you keep doing this? You don't even like drinking.

I messed it all up, peanut. I'm sorry.
I just ruin things and I don't deserve you.

Okay, enough of this silly "macho" pity party, Dad. Help me out. Use your legs.

Looks like we're only getting to the couch today. Good enough.
Sleep it off, and we'll have a little talk when I get home about how cheap whiskey doesn't fix anything.
I love you, Indy.

I know, Dad. That's why I'm still here.

Ohhhh no.

Crap.
Crap.
CRAP!

DINER
SLAM!

-huff- What are my tables today, Mel?!

Welcome! Did you get a chance to look at the menus?
INDIGO! Can I speak with you?

Third time this month you're late.
I know, sir, I was helping my dad...
Who do you think covers your shift while we're waiting for you?

Nobody wants excuses, young lady.

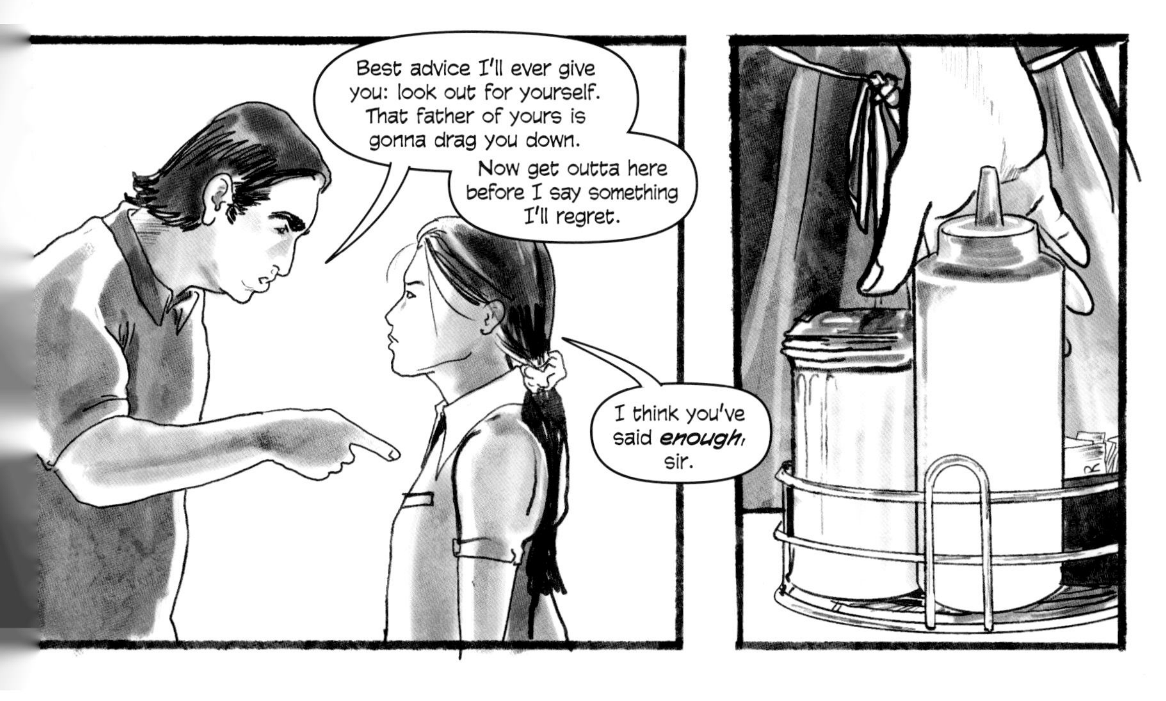
Best advice I'll ever give you: look out for yourself. That father of yours is gonna drag you down.
Now get outta here before I say something I'll regret.
I think you've said enough, sir.

¡#@$&!!
Well, not the day I was expecting to have so far...

COFFEE FIXES EVERYTHING

COFFEE FIXES EVERYTHING

Hope there's enough room in my bag for this mess.
TRASH
Oh, no.

That is the LAST person I need to see right now.

Indigo! I thought that was you.

Deb!
Look! Your stepdaughter's here!

Ex-stepdaughter, Marjean. But yes, look, *here she is.*

You must just be getting off your shift at that greasy diner. And in that polyester nightmare. *Good for you*.
I was just saying to Marjean the other day how I was worried about you without a strong female role model in your life.

That's true. Deb is *such* a dedicated mother. It pains me not to see her and your *handsome* father about town anymore. They were like our very own Hollywood couple.
Um... *okay*. Oh! How is Rachel feeling, ma'am?

Isn't that kind of you to finally ask? We're having a fundraiser today for her next treatment in two weeks.
Rachel is still my fighting angel, bless her fragile little body. And I suppose it's a better environment for her now that it's just the two of us.
I find strength in being her mother, you know. I'm equipped to take on that battle alone; I hope you're not letting your father be too much of a burden, now that he's all your responsibility?

Say something! How dare she talk about Dad like that?!
Stand up to her. Don't just stand there like an idiot!
Um... *no* ma'am.
I... I have to go.
What was THAT? You coward.
You might stop by the powder room on your way out.
Bless your heart, I think there's foo on your face.
Oh COME on!

THE QUARRY

SPLASH!

Today sucks.

Hey, Indigo, come jump in the lake! There's too many dudes in here.
Go ask your mom, Jimmy.

Whatever, you're not *all that*.
Jimmy, chill.

Nobody wants to be seen with the town trash anyway.

WHAM!

I knew you'd go *postal* one of these days.
Let's bounce, Tom.

Hmm, the trash still has a pretty good arm.

You're lucky you have donuts or you'd be next!

So what's the emergency? I came right over after I finished my morning shift.

I got fired, Kasia. I woke up late again, and my dad was drunk at the table.
My whole life is just self-destructing.

I can't sleep, my dad's a mess, and now I don't even have a job.

Oh, Indigo, I'm sorry.
And you know what the worst part is?
What?

We've gotta get your other shoe.
Huh?

Oh.
oh No NOo!

SPLASH!

LATER
I'll talk to my mom tonight. I won't be able to work as many hours during my internship, so maybe you could take those shifts.
That's really nice of you, Kasia. I'm gonna miss seeing as much of you, but it's so cool you're gonna be a surgeon.

Hah! That won't be for a long, long time. And I'll always have time for you, Indy.
My super smart best friend is going to college in the fall, and things are changing so fast.
I don't even know what I'm doing with my life...

You're gonna find your thing, Indy, I swear.
I better head home, it's getting dark.

Okay, call you tomorrow, Kasia.

Dad?
You still
home?

In here, peanut.
Just getting ready
for work.

How was
your shift
today?

Ugh.
Don't
ask.
That bad,
huh?
Nobody
tipped?

I got
fired.

Oh no...

This is all my
fault...

Stop playing the victim, Dad. I don't wanna hear it tonight!
I'm just sorry I keep messing up your life, Indy.
If you want to go live with your aunt in Poughkeepsie, maybe it's better for you.

Stop trying to run away from your problems, Dad. You're acting like the person Deb makes you out to be.

Just *fight* for once!
SLAM!

Dammit, Indy. Can you control your emotions, like, ever?

..sniff..

What the--?

Umm...

What is happening to my *life?*

2

Connection

Hey, Kas-
There wasn't a freak windstorm last night, was there?
No, huh? And you're totally sure?

I'm just glad you gave me the afternoon shift to start at the donut shop.
I barely slept at all again.
THE UGL
ACKALOPES
TAP TAP

Listen, can you meet me at the quarry? I want to talk to you about something first...

20 MINUTES LATER
What's up, weirdo, first day of work jitters? You know my dad is only a *little* scary.

I know I'm going to sound crazy, but I just have to say it.
I... think I'm being haunted.

Oookay. Explain this conclusion, please.
You know it's been no mystery that I can't sleep.
I've done all the research -- I know about sleep paralysis and how it messes with your mind.
But last night my whole room was trashed. Like a poltergeist or a nightmare troll came in and wrecked it. And I felt trapped in my body for the whole thing.

There's something more going on, and I just don't know how much longer I can take it.
Indy, I'm so sorry. I know you've been exhausted, and life really has been unfair lately.
But... I have an idea! Make it through this first shift and I'll be by after class.
Also, I just washed my hair, so if you blow your sad dandelion near me you won't even *make it* to your first shift to hear my brilliant plan.
INDY!!!

Even though I have sugar coming out of every pore of my body, this is still *way* better than the diner.
Free DONUT on your Birthday!
How was class? And what's this plan on how you're going to pull me back from the brink of insanity?

Well, your problem sounded familiar, like something I heard of a long time ago.
You know how I always solve things...

With a book!

SPRINKLE
sigh

Oh, look at that, you solved all my problems. You found a way to put me to sleep. I'll just go home now.

C'mon, Indy! It's all right here. I remembered the folk stories my mom told me as a child. You have a Mare!

Great, okay. Wake me up when you're done reading to me.

Nie prowokuj mnie! You asked for help, this is it.

According to the stories, it says that a ***Mare*** is someone who was wronged, or a rejected woman who visits in the night. They sneak in and drain you in your sleep.
But there's also a list of ways to ward them off or protect yourself.
We've got a whole week of ideas here!

And so...
Here goes *Experiment* Day 1.
First one is easy! It says to drink coffee grounds before bed.
DONUT
Already on that one!
I'm terrible at making coff There's alway grounds in it
Sooo jittery...

Okay, what about "sleeping with a leather"?
I guess that means a belt?
Ugh.

Next!

"You can confuse the Mare by sleeping upside down..."

Meh.

"...or by putting a broom upside down or a bird at your door..."

"Try inviting the Mare to breakfast."

"Some fill
eir bed with
ay and hide
n another
room."

STASH'S
Oh. *Instant* regret.
ACHOO

COMBO DEAL
ANY JELLY DONUT
MAPLE LOG $1
GLAZED
BLUEBERRY
PEACH COBBLER
PEANUT BUTTER
CAKE
CHERRY
CAPPUCHINO
Okay, "Try to steal the Mare's hat."
Hm, that won't work. What else do we have...
"Smear feces upon your fron door."

No!
This is done. "Experiment Day whatever-it-is," game's over. Line is drawn at poop!

Please. I know your m can prescribe sleeping pills. I need one full ni of sleep befor completely lose it.

Ugh -- *no.* I don't like that idea. Let's try something else.

My dad can close up. Time for a field trip.

Where are we going?
To my favorite place!

Time for a little research.
I've never been here.
Oh, honey, I know.

Let's see who lived in your house before you and your dad.

Why?
We've ruled out a house demon. Maybe it's an old-fashioned haunting.

And you can find that out here?
We can look at old microfiche and see if there are any unsolved murders in our town. Every town has secrets.
Geez, there *are* unsolved cases.
So many missing women and children... But nothing with your dad's address.
All these vulnerable people have been missing for years and we've never even heard about them. It's so sad, isn't it?

Indy?
Oh, Indy.

Okay, let's go see my mom.
I hate resorting to a pill, but you can't do another day like this.

Kasia's right.

I hate resorting to this too.

But one good night's sleep...

Maybe that's all I need to set me back on track?
Cross your paws for me, One Eye.

BAM
BANG
BAM
BANG

Ow!
Crap.
What the hell!?

So now I sleepwalk?

Better stay on the ground floor until these pills wear off. Geez. Glad Dad's at work. I guess.
Can't wait to see ... what bruises pop up tomorrow... morni...

Get outta the road, freak!!

Huh?

Deb's house?
How did -- WHY did I walk all the way across town?

I know I used to live here, but...
Why is my face wet?

Oh Jesus, Indy, get home before anybody sees you out here like this.

Bulletproof

...I wish I was

THE NEXT DAY

But are you *sure* you're out of maple bars?
Yes, I'm *sure* we're out of them because Stash doesn't make maple bars.

aybe you could out suggestion cards.
STASH'S DONUTS
I'll be sure to suggest that, Stanley.

Oh hello, I've been told the maple bars are really good here.
Very funny, asshole.

I'm sorry, that was totally uncalled for.
I even slept last night. Kind of.

That's great news, Indy! So what's the matter?
Stanley has never gotten under your skin before. You usually love how weird he is.

Yeah, I know. Things last night, they... got out of control. Sleeping pills are not my answer.
What do you mean? What happened?

I sleepwalked across town and woke up in front of my old house covered in orange soda.

Oh.

I know. My reality is either I am tortured all night, totally locked in a... state... or I pass out cold and *hit the town.*
Sugar

Fun options, right?
JELLY

Did your book say anything about curses? 'Cause that's how I feel.

Could someone be trying to contact you from beyond the grave?

I don't know, Kas... this all just feels so crazy and out of control.

C'mere.
CLUNK
Watch the coffee.

I almost forgot! I've got a surprise to completely fix everything...

TWO TICKETS TO ***THE UGLY JACKALOPES***, THIS FRIDAY NIGHT!

No.
WAY.
You are the best. I don't deserve a friend like you!
And now you *really* have to make a tape for me. Rachel still has my CD at Deb's house and I'm *not* showing up there again!

Oh crap.

Oh geez, sorry, Indy. Guess you spoke too soon!

Hate to run -- I have class!
Don't kill me for running out on this mess!
Ha! Just don
forget my tap
tomorrow!

Hmph...

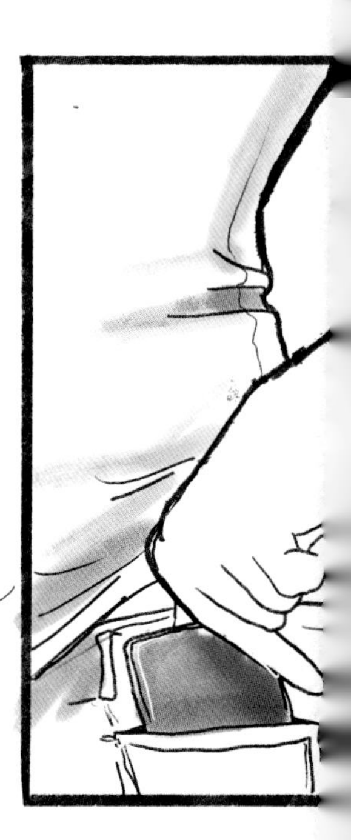

DRIVER LICENSE
SAT AUG 07,1993
THE CHANCE

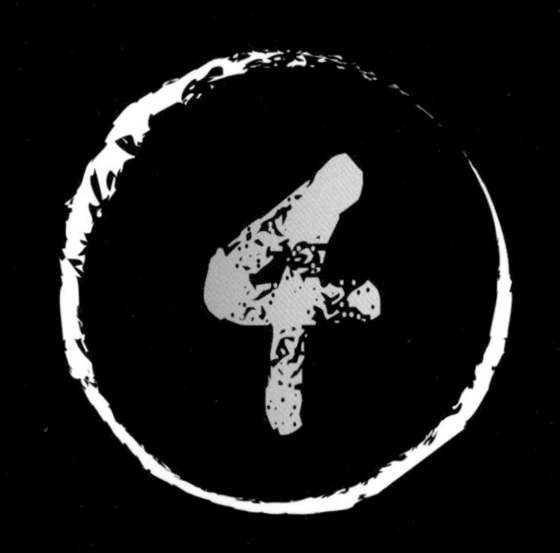
4

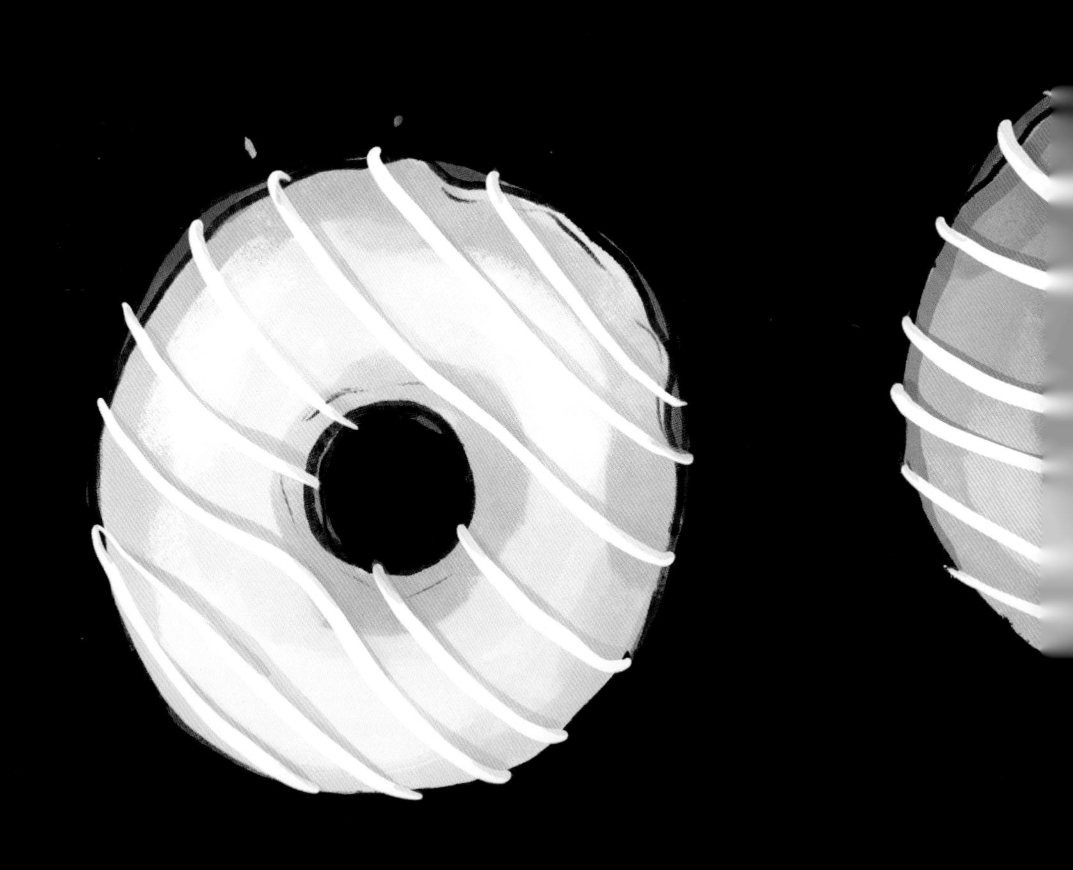

Heart-Shaped Box

(of donuts)

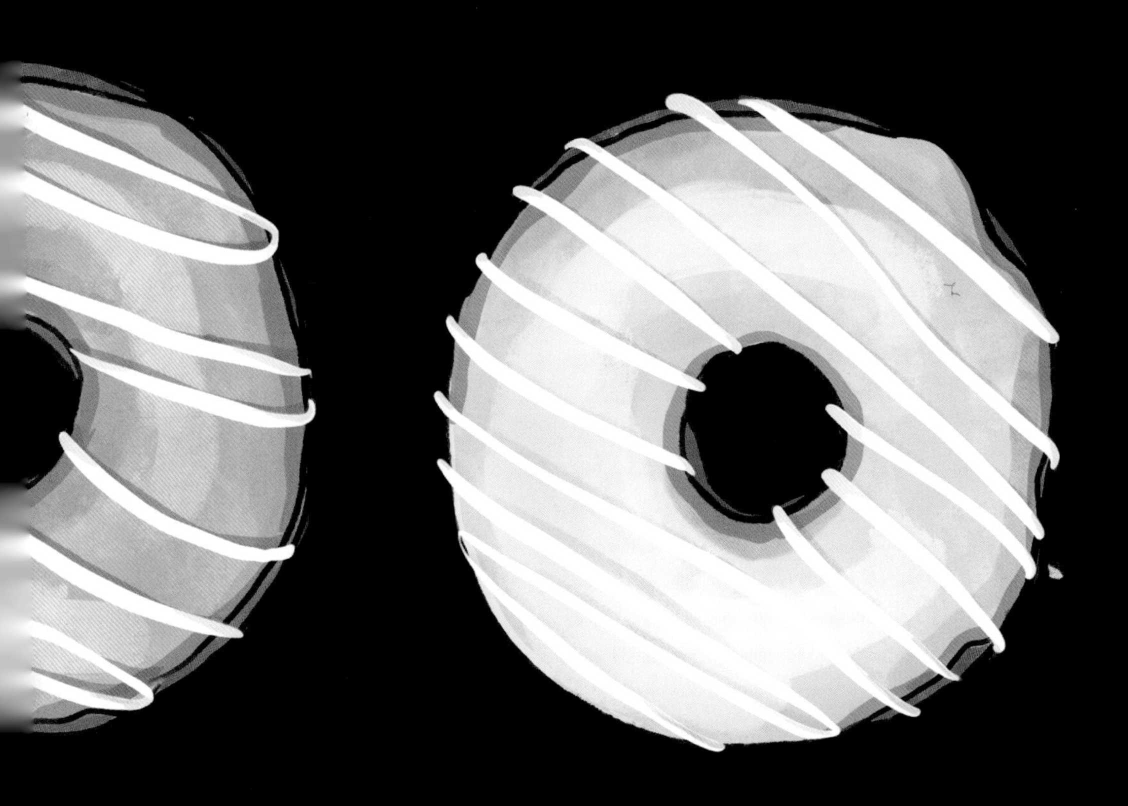

Afternoon shifts are so slow this time of year.
BLACK CHERRY
BLUEBERRY LEMON
BLACK + WHITE

BLACK CHERRY
BLUEBERRY LEMON
BLACK + WHITE

CLOSED
Thank You! Come Again

ON
OFF

HELP
HELP ME

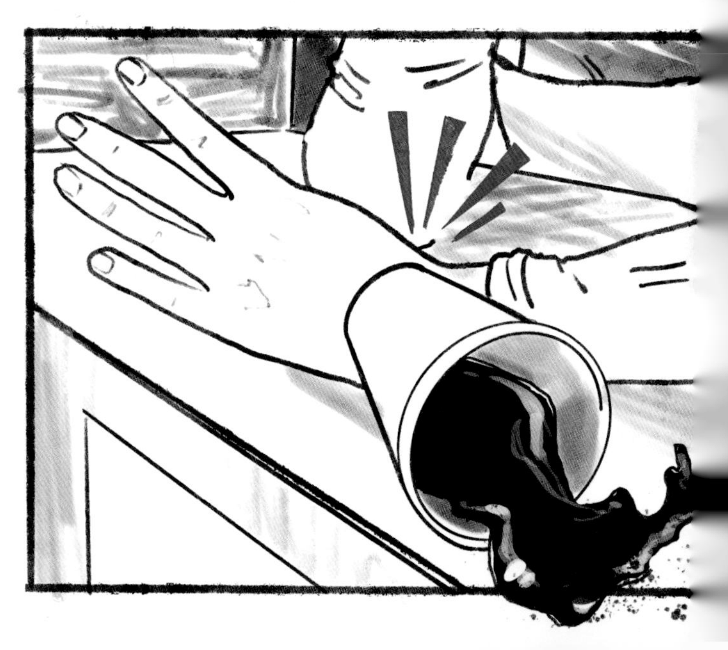

Sorry! I, uh-- oh, it's *you*.
You threw your coffee everywhere, and you almost soaked me!

Just gimme a *black coffee*.

sigh

Sorry... I ... I didn't mean to, like, scare you or whatever.
It gets dark so early and I'm tired too.
So, like, I was an asshole this summer. I'm trying to get my shit together. My mouth... just gets ahead of me.

Yeah, well...
I *might* know a little bit about that myself.

On the house, Jimmy. Truce?
Truce!

Hey, you going to the Ugly Jackalopes show?

Yeah, me and Kasia are going.

Cool. Maybe I'll see you there.
Yo, I gotta bounce but this coffee spill is crazy...

...looks like a message or something.

5

THE UGLY
JACKALOPES

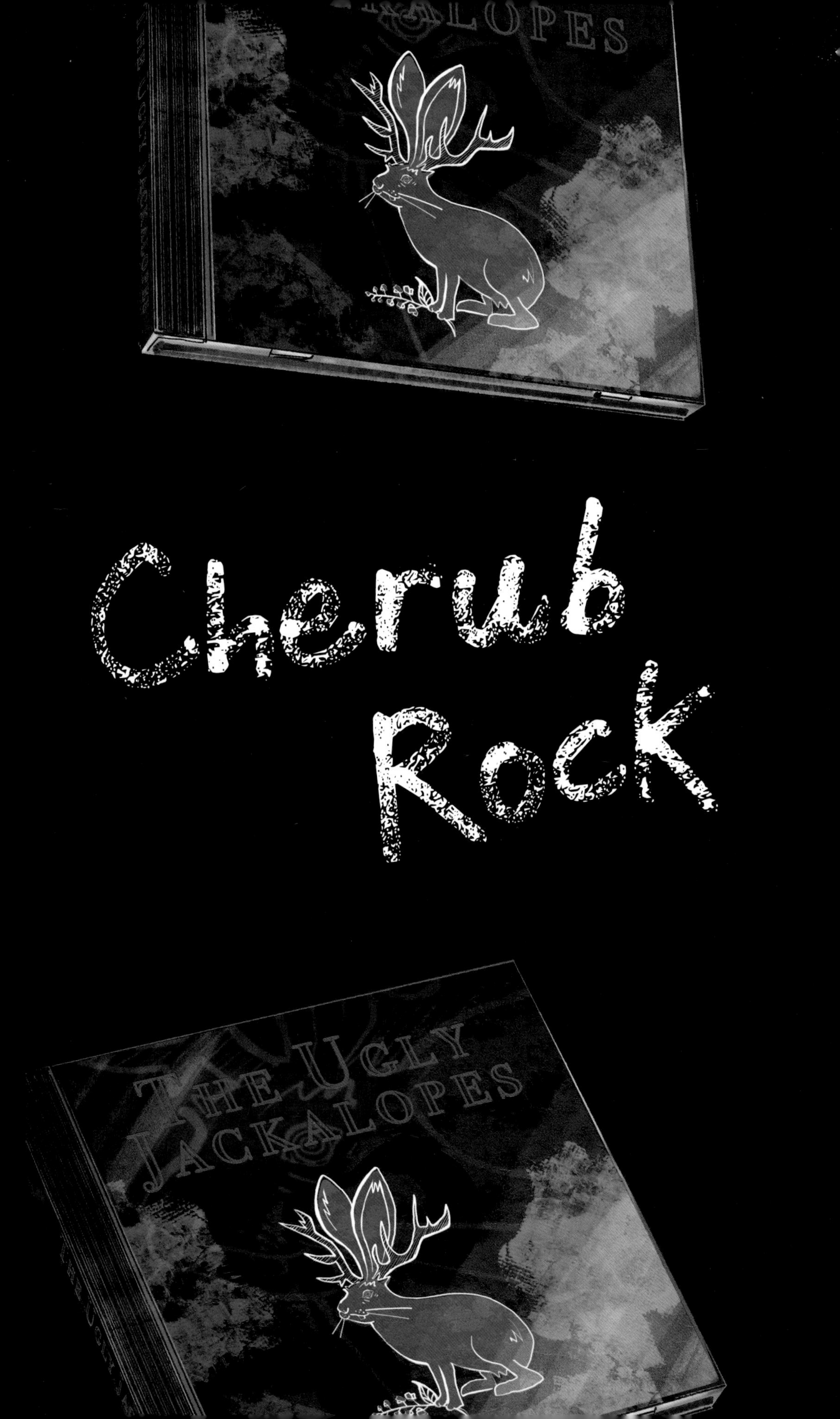
Cherub
Rock
THE UGLY
JACKALOPES

A FEW WEEKS LATER...
C'mon, Indy, we already missed the opener.

Who cares?!
I don't have anything cool to wear!

You got a new haircut and I just look like my usual sleep-deprived, tragic self.

Maybe I could just, like, tear the sleeves off this...

This is getting ridiculous.

Ew. Also, this stinks. Indy, when's the last time you did laundry?

UGHHH forget it!
Go without me!

We don't have time for this.

No... no... okay.

Put that on.

Maybe I don't look like barf in this?

Better than barf!
Now get in the dang car.

C'mon, we gotta push up front!

Yo, ladies and all you pathetic psychos, get ready for THE UGLY JACKALOPES!

Oh. Hey.
?

Holy crap, that was amazing! I swear my eardrums are totally broken and I just don't care!
I made eye contact with Drummer Steve. I think he definitely wants to marry me now.

You know what, Kas, I haven't felt this much like myself in a long time.
I've just been... floating. I know I've been tired and the lack of sleep makes me suck, but... I need my life to mean *something*.

It's cool how you know what you want to do with your life, K. How did you know?

Well, you know Tata Stash didn't give me much choice, but I always wanted to help people. Studying medicine made sense for me.

You don't have to figure it out yet, Indy. I just know we can all do a little good in our lives.

Thanks... for everything You're pretty o you know tha

Home sweet home.

Best ever Mix Tape by

Wow, it's been a while since I've said that.

What's gotten into me? It's almost like I'm... like, happy.

I think Kasia might be right; maybe I don't have to figure it all out yet. It's okay to just breathe and... not be a jerk.

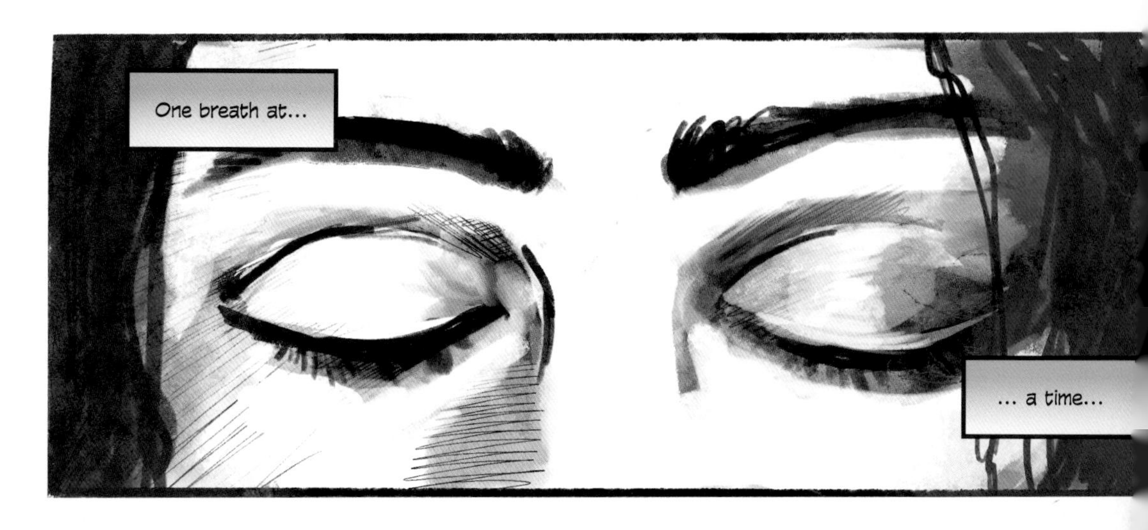
One breath at...
... a time...

No!

Not anymore.

I can stop this.

I can feel its icy grip.

Not going to let it happen *anymore!*

Wait...

That was *amazing*. Am I awake?
And if I am...

What the heck is that?

Why am I not scared?
Something feels...
like... familiar.

M-mom?

NO.
Holy crap!
Rachel??

Rachel? What are you doing here?

Rachel?

But I don't understand!

I don't understand!

Holy crap!

That felt so real.
Rachel?

Geez, that's a bruise!

The mixtape Rachel made me?
A
I swear I didn't leave it there.

I gotta talk to Rachel.

Good morning, ma'am.
This is Indigo. Can I please talk to Rachel?

Indigo. My little angel doesn't have the energy to talk on the phone. We've been at the doctor's all morning.
Quite frankly, it's rather inconsiderate of you to ask me to even bother her with your call.

I'm sorry, ma'am, I was just worried about her, could I just please --

Worried? You haven't cared about Rachel in months, and now you're worried?
Young lady, worry about yourself and your no-good father. Leave **us** alone.

Okay! That sure went well.
Way to go, Indy.

THE NEXT DAY
You know it's a bad idea, Indy.
Deb won't change her mind.
STASHS

I'm sure everything is fine. Right?
It was just your crazy dreams.
But...
What if it's *not*? What if she needs you for real?

But... I gotta try.

Oh hey, little kitty!

Not kitty!

This was a **bad idea**.

KNOCK KNOCK

CLICK

Hi, ma'am, *Deb*, I'm sorry --

Sorry?
No, clearly you are NOT sorry!
Showing up at my front door in the middle of the night? You must be HIGH! I can smell it all over you!
Middle of the-- ? It's not even 7:30! Hold your ground, Indy. C'mon.

Deb -- I'm not *high* -- there was a skunk, please can I just --
Bloodshot eyes, and you can't even string together a sentence.
I don't need a degenerate like you near *my daughter*! She sees her doctor tomorrow and needs REST.
Show up here again, and I'm calling the police!

SLAM

Stop beating yourself up, Indy. That woman just doesn't like you or your dad.
It's not worth picking a fight. She'll win. Everyone in this stupid town thinks she's the local saint and hero mom.
Well, they're wrong. She's fake and no one notices while she hides behind Rachel.
I'm just worried about Rachel. What if something's super weird? Does she have, like, super powers?

I know that dream really affected you and I'm glad you shared it with me. We have to figure this out.

Where do I even start? I can't do this.

I'm gonna do a little digging when I'm doing my internship at the hospital tomorrow.
And Indy, don't be ridiculous.

You're strong, you're smart. You'll get through this.

THE NEXT DAY
Oh hey, Kas, what's up?

I gotta whisper, Indy, so listen closely.
I pulled Rachel's files, and Deb only allowed one doctor to come for home visits.
She doesn't have an appointment today. Or any on the books.

Rachel hasn't actually been seen in almost six months.

Indy?

6

Best ever Mix Tape by Rachel
A

Little Earthquakes

Hey, you. Interesting place to meet.
This is where Rachel played soccer. This is the normal life she *should* be having.

There must be a good explanation why Deb hasn't brought Rachel to her doctor's appointments, right?

I don't understand anything about that woman. She pretends to be so perfect in public and then she's wretched behind closed doors.

When she and my dad first got married, she acted like I was family. Rachel and I got along like sisters. I mean, sometimes we fought, but whatever.
That's, like, normal, right?
Once she got bored of my dad and started cheating on him, she made sure to tell everyone he drank too much. And he didn't -- well, back then.
Finally, when she ended things, it felt so *forbidden* to call Rachel. When Rach got sick, Deb would tell people I never called, but the few times I tried, she wouldn't let us talk.

I just wish I'd tried harder. I was so wrapped up in my own problems...

No way. This is not on you, Indy. You just need to talk to Rachel *somehow*, and everything will sort itself out.
You should just drop one of those leftover sleeping pills into her royal highness's evening martini. She couldn't stop you if she was snoozing.

!

Ah, Kas, um, I gotta go!
Ugh, *don't wanna do this...*

Indy? Hey, uh, *I WAS JUST KIDDING!*

Oh, Indy, please don't do something stupid.

POP

AHHH!

You terrible girl, creeping around at night like a common criminal!

I *knew* you were on drugs! Just you wait, the sheriff will throw the book at you!

Wha-- WHAT ARE YOU DOING??

SET ME FREE
No. It can't be you.

YOU WENT TOO FAR

No.
This is all a trick. You're not real.

You stay away from me, whatever you are!

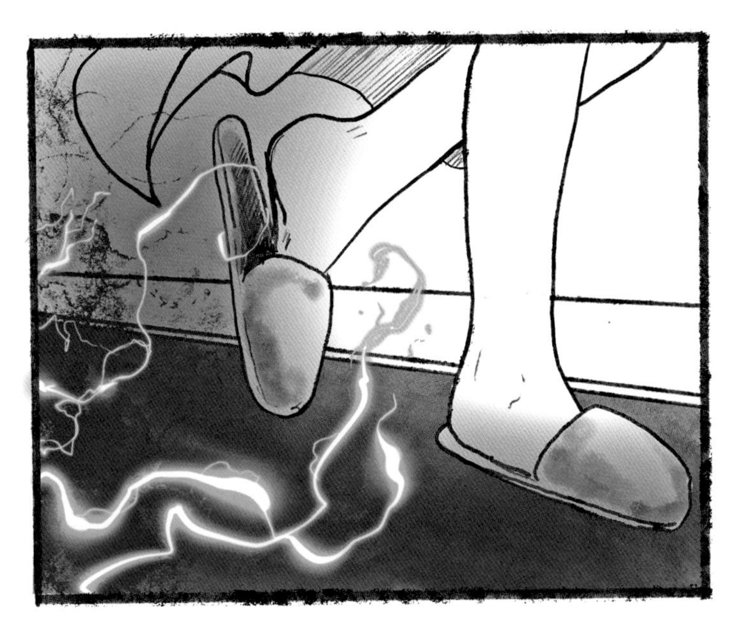

The police will come for you!
LET THEM COME

STAY
AWAY!

WHY, MOTHER?

No!
NO!!
YOU KEPT ME SICK EVERY DAY

WAS IT WORTH IT? MY HEALTH FOR THE MONEY AND ATTENTION?

YOU WENT TOO FAR

I just needed...
this *pathetic* town to know how much *better than them* we are.
I was doing it for ***us***.
I... didn't mean to *take it* so far...

BUT YOU DID

Oh god, my baby.
I'm sorry.
I'm so, so sorry.

TOO LATE FOR SORRY

IT'S ALL OVER

NOW MAKE THE CALL

AND LET ME GO

THANK YOU, INDY

I'M SORRY... FOR EVERYTHING
YOU WERE MY LAST CONNECTION. I WAS LOST, ANGRY, AND CONFUSED
I HAD NO HOPE, BUT YOU WERE STRONG

THERE ARE MORE OUT THERE SUFFERING LIKE I ... WAS
HELP THEM
YOU MAY NOT REMEMBER THIS MOMENT, BUT REMEMBER THEY NEED YOU. NOW GO--

SISTER
EMT

EPILOGUE

Dreams

Heya, Pops! Cold out there!

Hey, peanut! Good thing I've got dinner hot and ready.

How was school?
I mean, not bad. I have so much to learn.

I'm so glad Kasia convinced me to take this class.
The professor was telling us today that it was only just recently signed into law for the government to create a database to help track child abusers.

Can you believe that? It feels like something that should have existed for, like, ever.
I believe it, Indy. There are a lot of bad people out there, and only people who give a damn can change that.

Welp, off I go. These roads aren't gonna plow themselves.

Hey, peanut.
I'm proud you're one of those people who actually gives a damn.

Night, Dad.

Open Me for TRACK LIST

Best Ever Mix Tape by Rachel

INTRODUCTION TO CRIMINAL JUSTICE
INTRODUCTION TO CRIMINAL JUSTICE
JUSTICE

NTRODUCTION
TO CRIMINAL
JUSTICE
ALARM
PM
11:09

STEREO

Best ever Mix Tape by Rachel

A (This tape is soooOoooOOO much better than any tape you will ever ~~[illegible]~~ get your ears will thank me)

cuz nobody loves me its true

1. Sour Times — Portishead
2. Connection — elastica
3. Bulletproof I Wish I was... — Radiohead
4. Heart Shaped Box — Nirvana
5. Cherub Rock — Smashing Pumpkins
6. Little Earthquakes — Tori!
7. Dreams — Cranberries

BONUS

Wild Indigo (your fave - It may cut off cuz there are so many GOOD songs) — The Ugly Jackalopes

end

THE UGLY
ACKALOPES
ALL AGES
9pm / $ 10
AY OCT 13
STAGE
DOOR
BANDS
ONLY

If you or someone you know is being abused or neglected, here are some resources to help.

CHILDHELP NATIONAL CHILD ABUSE HOTLINE
Call or text: 1-800-422-4453
childhelphotline.org

THE NATIONAL CENTER FOR MISSING
& EXPLOITED CHILDREN
24-hour hotline: 1-800-THE-LOST
missingkids.org

For more information and resources on child welfare, including how to spot abuse or help with a personal situation:
CHILD WELFARE INFORMATION GATEWAY
childwelfare.gov

If you or someone else is in immediate and serious danger, you should call 911.

Anyone can report suspected child abuse or neglect. Reporting abuse or neglect can protect a child and get help for a family.

While this story is fictional, it depicts a very real psychopathology known as Munchausen Syndrome by Proxy, specifically Factitious Disorder Imposed on Another (FDIA). For more information, see munchausensupport.com/faq/.

Other guidance can be found via The American Professional Society on the Abuse of Children: apsac.org/9235fgnl8.

Thank you to my house of gingers for holding dow[n] the fort, picking up the slack, and keeping me san[e] while I was creating this